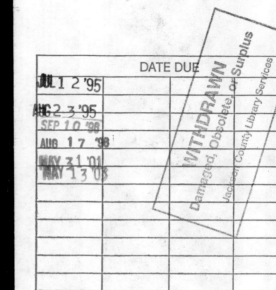

Jackson

County

Library

Services

HEADQUARTERS:

413 W. Main

Medford, Oregon 97501

WHO IS MY NEIGHBOR?

by Michael Grejniec

AN UMBRELLA BOOK
Alfred A. Knopf · New York

I live on the edge of town. The sky is always cloudy here. The streets are always gray.

No one else lives in my building– except for the man upstairs.

I used to watch him through my window. He'd leave at the same time every morning. He'd come back at the same time every evening.

I could never see his face. It made me
a little afraid.
Who **is** my neighbor? I would wonder.

One night our electricity went out. "Phil, go upstairs and borrow some candles from Mr. Hart," my mother said.

"Why me?" I asked myself, climbing higher and higher.

I knocked on the door.

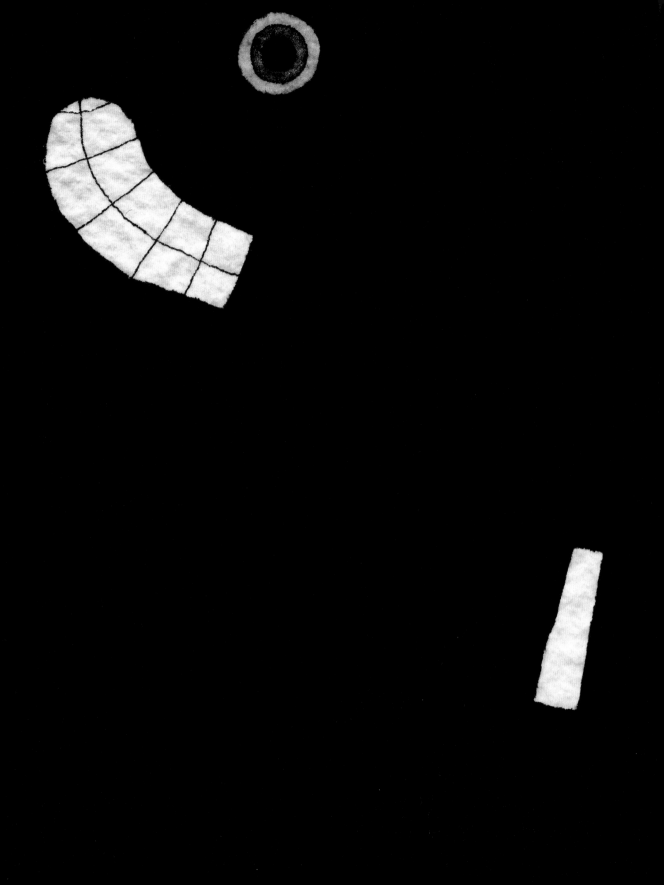

When it opened, all I could see was a smile and eyes.

"Can I borrow a candle?" I asked.

"Please come in," said my neighbor's voice.

Get me out of here, I thought.

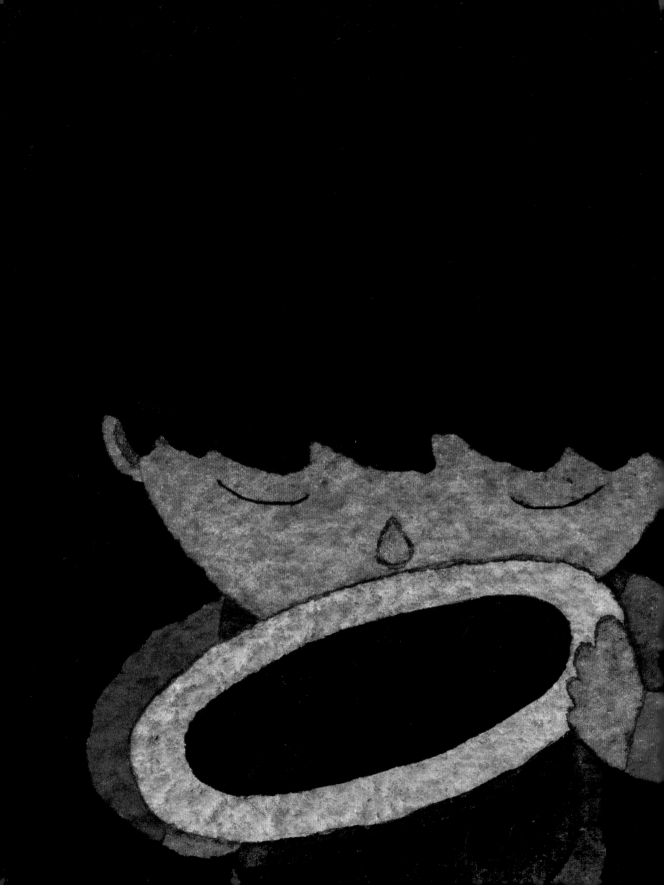

I didn't see any furniture, except for a table.
On the table was a hat.
"Look inside," said my neighbor.
Was that where he kept his candles?
But I found nothing.
Then he reached in.

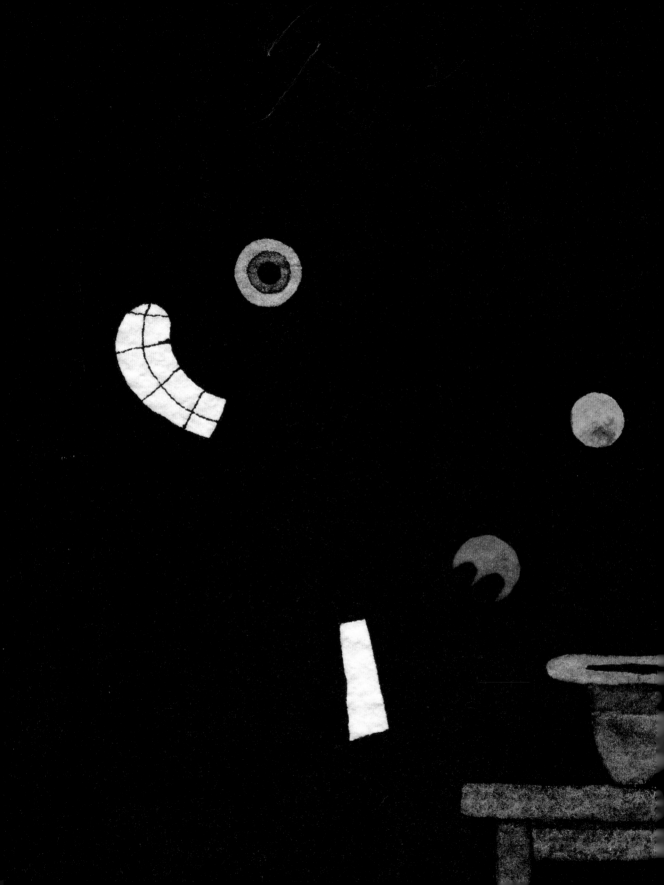

"Catch!" he said, and pulled out a bright yellow ball. Next came a blue one...a green one...a red one.

My neighbor reached in the hat again, and
out hopped one…two…three rabbits! I tried
to pet them, but they hopped away.
    "Neigh-h-h-h!"

A horse pranced out, and I jumped on its back. Around and around we rode, till I got so dizzy I had to get off. **"Roar-r-r-r!"**

I was on a lion's back! "How did I get here, anyway?" I asked as we leapt through a ring of fire.
Ouch!

An elephant was squeezing me with his trunk as he lifted me onto a trapeze. I grabbed hold and swung higher and higher. Then I let go. **Wheeee!**

I flew through the air and came down
on a round full moon. I jumped to a half
moon…to a quarter moon…

...and then to just a sliver of a moon. Down and down I slid, till at last I landed...

...**boom!** on the ground. All around me my
neighbor's room was swirling, a flying circus
filled with magic. Was I dreaming?

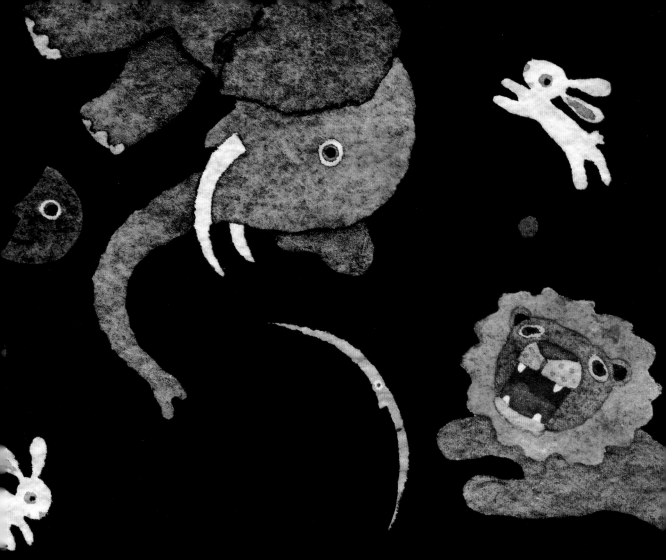

There was my neighbor, smiling down at me.
I remembered why I had come.
   "Can I borrow a candle?" I asked again.
   "Look inside now," he said.
I reached in the hat.

Inside, I found a twinkling star.
My neighbor let me take it home.

Now we had light. Everything was brighter
than it had ever been.

I still watch my neighbor walk down the street every morning and come home every evening. From my window the sky looks less cloudy, and the streets look less gray. My neighbor waves to me, and I wave back.

I hope I can visit him again soon.

For Mette–my imaginary friend

–M. G.

AN UMBRELLA BOOK PUBLISHED BY ALFRED A. KNOPF, INC.

Text and illustrations copyright © 1994 by Michael Grejniec
All rights reserved under International and Pan-American Copyright Conventions.
Published in the United States of America by Alfred A. Knopf, Inc., New York, and
simultaneously in Canada by Random House of Canada Limited, Toronto.
Distributed by Random House, Inc., New York.

Library of Congress Cataloging-in-Publication Data
Grejniec, Michael.
Who is my neighbor? / by Michael Grejniec.
p.   cm. — (An Umbrella book)
Summary: A young boy discovers that his upstairs neighbor has some
very special talents.
ISBN 0-679-85801-6 (trade) — ISBN 0-679-95801-0 (lib. bdg.)
[1. Neighborliness—Fiction. 2. Magicians—Fiction.] I. Title.
II. Series: Umbrella books.
PZ7.G8625Who   1994
[E]—dc20   93-39248

Manufactured in the United States of America
2 4 6 8 0 9 7 5 3 1

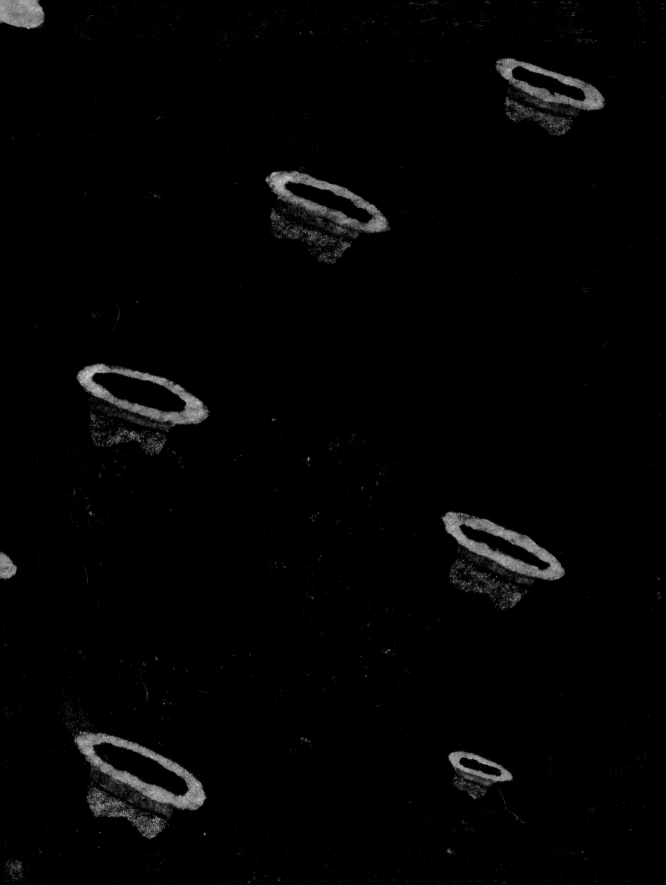